MERLE THE HIGH FLYING SQUIRREL

BILL PEET

HOUGHTON MIFFLIN COMPANY BOSTON/1974

FOR PAUL

Library of Congress Cataloging in Publication Data

Peet, Bill.
Merle the high flying squirrel.

SUMMARY: Unhappy about the noise and clutter of the city, a squirrel travels west to find peace and quiet in the forest of giant trees he has heard about.
(1. Squirrel — Fiction) I. Title.
PZ10.3.P2989Me (E) 73-18371

ISBN: 0-395-18452-5 (Rnf)
ISBN: 0-395-34923-0 (Pa)

Printed in the United States of America
Y 10 9 8 7

Merle was a scrawny young squirrel who lived in a big city park up in an oak tree. He was such a timid frightened little squirrel, he hardly ever came down out of the tree. The noisy traffic made him jittery and the towering gray buildings gave him the creeps. And the people who came to the park frightened him even though most of them were friendly. Whenever someone offered Merle a peanut, he kept at a safe distance until they tossed it to him. Then in a flash, he was back up the tree.

RAMONA
KATHY
TIM
J.O.H.

"I'm tired of being scared," Merle said one morning. "It's no fun at all. From now on, I'm going to try and be brave. Even brave enough to take a trip somewhere. I might go all the way across the park and back."

That same morning, Merle overheard a group of men trading stories about all the places they had been and all the things they had seen. Since the little squirrel had never been anywhere, he loved stories about faraway places, and he pricked up his ears to catch every word. Then, without even knowing it, he left his tree to end up perched on a park bench right beside them.

"I've seen a lot of things," said one bearded old fellow, "but nothing ever got me like the big trees out in the West. Why some of them shoot up tall as the tallest building, and they're a heap sight more beautiful. When you are standin' there in amongst 'em, you get to feelin' mighty small. Not measly small like here in the city. It's a good feelin'. And there's a great quietness about 'em. Like as if those giant trees have been standin' there for thousands of years just storin' up quiet. But you've got to see 'em to understand what I mean."

After the men had gone, Merle sat up in the oak trying to imagine a tree as tall as a building.

HOTE

"I just can't believe it," he said. "Not until I see one. So I must take a trip out west, that's what. I don't dare run along the streets and highways. I'd get squashed in no time. The only safe way for a squirrel to travel is on the telephone wires, that is, if they go all the way out west. I wonder who would know?"

"Who would know what?" asked a goldfinch, fluttering down beside him.

"If the telephone wires go all the way out west?" said Merle.

"They go everywhere," said the finch. "So what?"

"So I'm going there," said the squirrel.

"But that's hundreds of miles," said the bird." "Way too much of a trip for a squirrel. It would take forever."

"Just the same," said Merle, "I'm going."

With a sad "good-bye" to his oak tree, Merle took a flying leap over to the nearest telephone wire. Then after making sure which way was west, he started off. High wire walking was something new for Merle, and at first he teetered along unsteadily. The rumble of traffic down below gave him the shakes, and he had to remind himself to be brave.

"Remember," he muttered, "no more being scared. I've got to be brave! Brave! Brave! Brave!" And just like that, Merle got over the shakes and was scampering along the wires at a fast lickety-clip.

"At this rate," he said, "the trip out west will be easy. I'll be there before I know it."

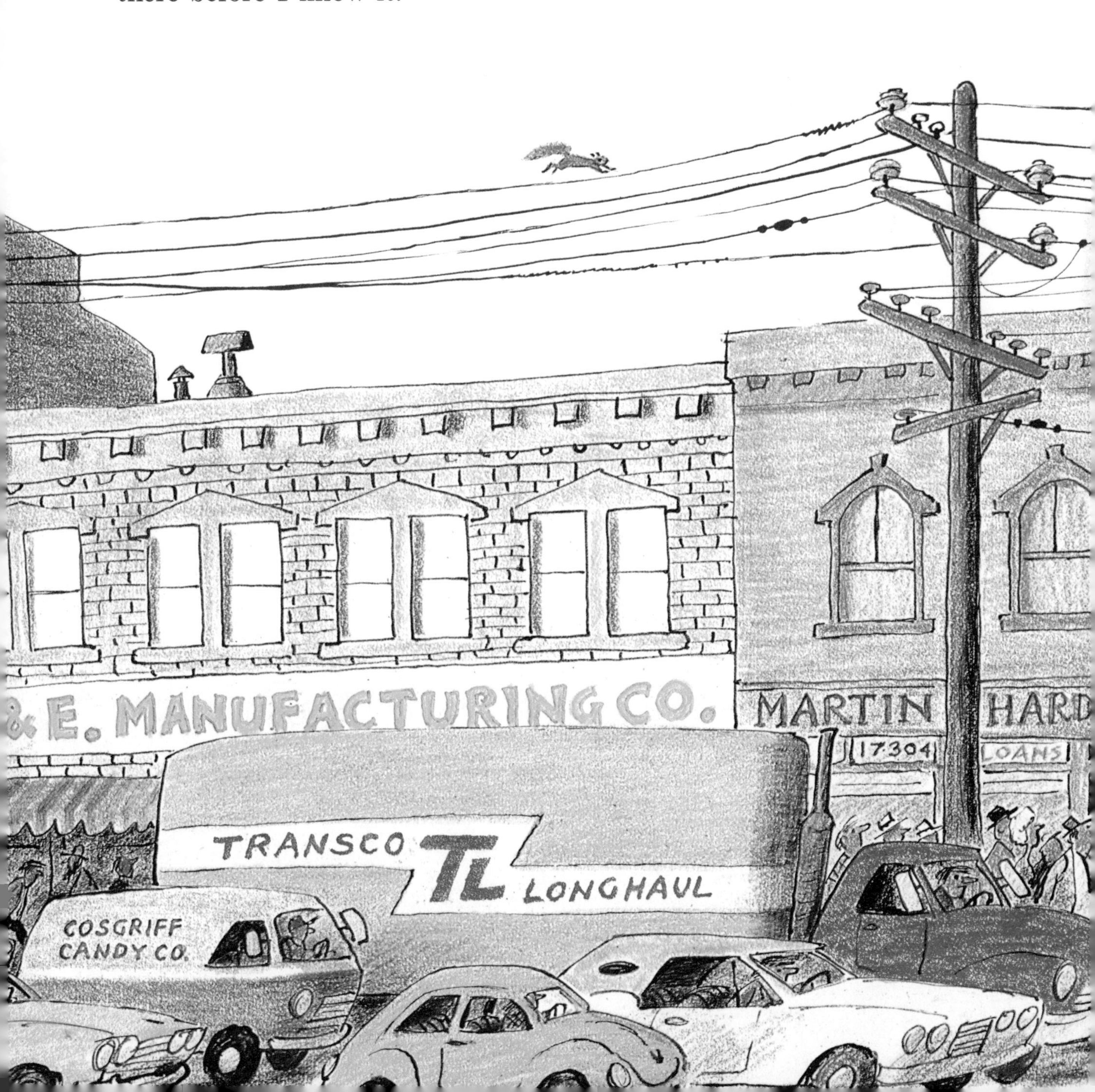

But before he knew it most of the day was gone. It was late afternoon and Merle was getting tired. And to his dismay, he was still in the city. Finally, he hopped to the top of a telephone pole to catch his breath and give his aching feet a rest. As the squirrel sat there staring at the buildings rising up in the hazy distance, suddenly he realized the trip was impossible.

"The bird was right," he sighed. "It is way too much of a trip for a squirrel. It would take forever."

So Merle gave up his dream of seeing the big trees and headed back for the park. By now, the sun was setting and it would be dark long before he reached the oak tree. So Merle began looking around for a safe place to spend the night.

Pretty soon he spied a big sign on a factory building, and in one leap, he was on the roof. Then, picking out a huge letter *S*, he curled up in the bottom curve and was sound asleep in a second.

NS

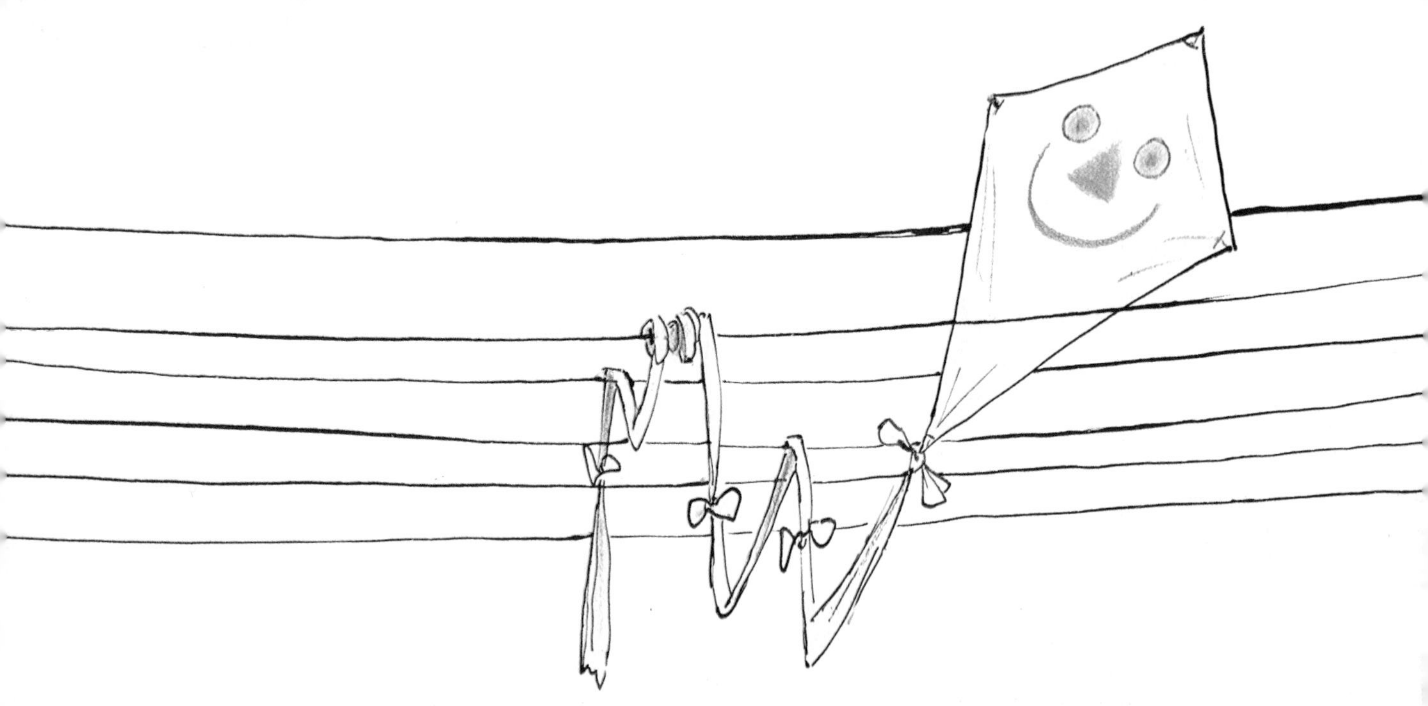

The next morning, Merle was awakened by voices coming from somewhere below, and he sat up with a shiver of fright.

"We could grab it by the tail," someone said, "if we could reach it. What we need is a tall, tall ladder."

In a flash, the squirrel was on top of the *S*. Then, peering down into the street, he spotted two boys. But they weren't looking at him. They were staring up at a kite with the tail tangled in the telephone wires.

"We need more than a ladder," said one boy. "We need a long pole, too. And I know where to find one. Let's go!"

As the boys raced away up the street, Merle got a bright idea.

"I'll surprise them," he said. "I'll untangle the tail and have the kite down before they get back."

Then he scurried out onto the wires and set to work. The squirrel was so busy tugging at the tangle, he didn't notice the storm clouds rolling over the city, or the first big rain drops pelting down. The fierce wind came up so quickly, Merle was caught by surprise, and *swoosh!* the kite was swept off the wires with the squirrel clinging tightly to the tail.

Suddenly, Merle was sailing high over the buildings on up into the boiling black clouds. Now he was *really* scared.

He feared the kite might be ripped to pieces, then down he would tumble into a street full of traffic. But the boys had made a good strong kite, and it sailed lightly along in the midst of the roaring, raging storm, smiling all the way.

For an instant, there was a break in the clouds and Merle caught a glimpse of the earth far below, a patchwork of fields with a tiny speck of a house and a barn here and there.

"I must be a mile high," thought Merle, "and going like sixty. I'm on a flying trip, and it might be a long one if I can just hang on."

And he tightened his grip on the wildly thrashing tail.

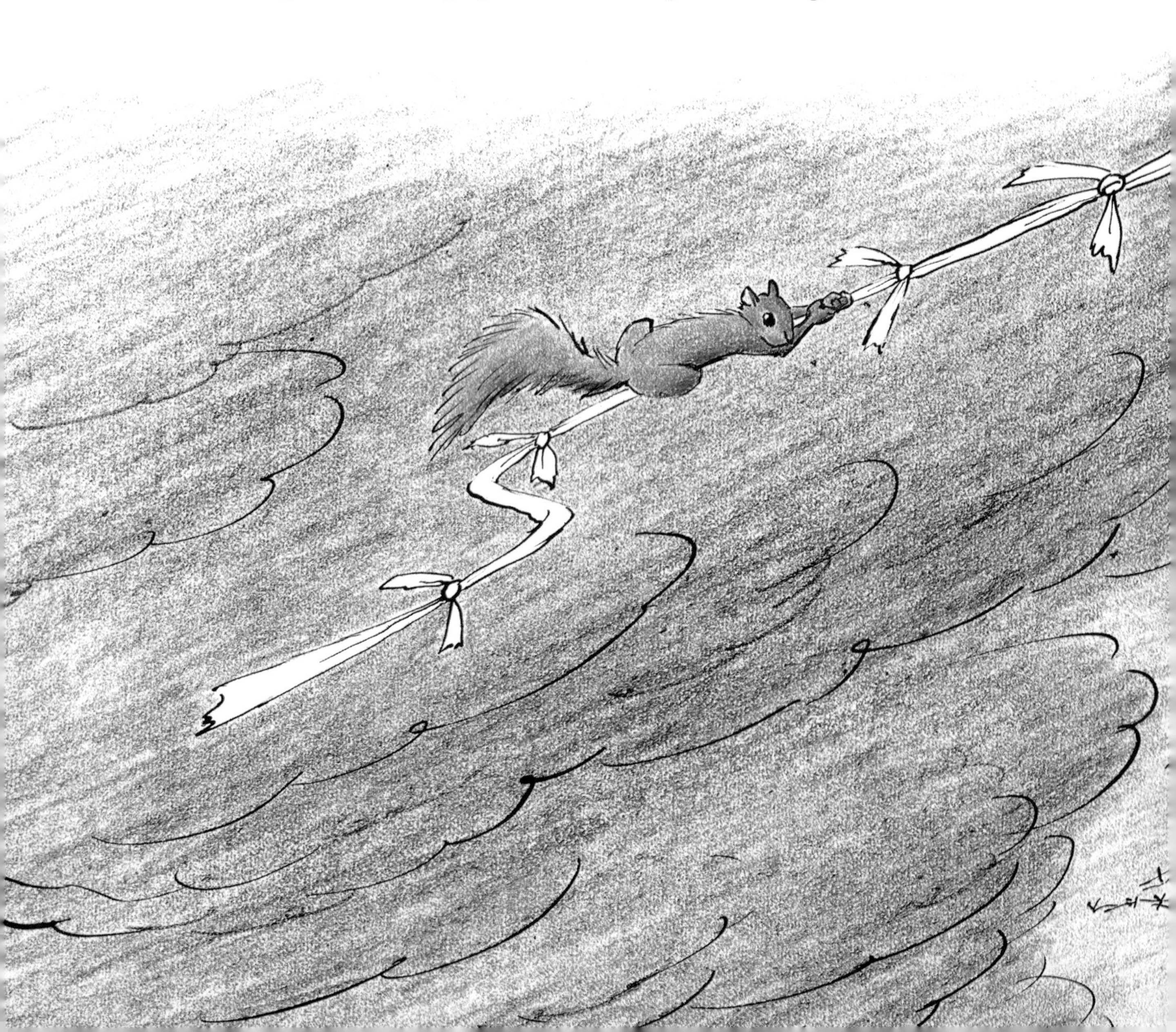

At last, the storm blew itself out, the wind died down to a whisper, and the kite dropped out of the clouds. The tail fell limp and the squirrel found himself drifting down into a barren wasteland of boulders and dry brush with no sign of a tree anywhere.

"No! No!" cried Merle, "not here! I couldn't stand to live here! Not even for a day!"

Just as the kite was settling to the ground, along came a whirlwind swirling up clouds of dust, thistles, and tumbleweeds. Finally, it caught the kite sending it into a tailspin, and Merle was taken for a dizzy, whirling ride straight up into the sky, higher than ever.

Then a powerful crosswind sent the kite sailing on into the afternoon over deep canyons and high above jagged mountain peaks. Beyond the mountains were dense pine forests, and the squirrel's eyes brightened.

"We've gone far enough," pleaded Merle, jerking frantically at the kite tail. "Come down, come down! You silly old kite!"

But the kite wasn't coming down. Not yet, anyway. The kite kept sailing for hours, carried along by a lively breeze high above more mountain peaks and more forests.

Then, just before sunset, the kite began drifting down through rosy pink clouds. The great red ball of a sun was slipping past the horizon casting its bright reflection across the broad shimmering sea. Suddenly the squirrel realized he had made the trip out west. Too far out west! The kite was heading out to sea!!

"I'm done for," groaned Merle. "This is the end of me for sure."

All at once, the kite stopped with a jerk. The tail had snagged onto the tip of a scraggly runt of a pine, and after one last flip-flop, it tumbled into the tree. And with a sigh of relief, the bedraggled squirrel hopped down to a branch for a look around.

In all directions a ghostly blanket of fog covered the ground with here and there a runt of a pine.

"What a weird place," muttered Merle, "but at least I'm lucky to land in a tree and not in the sea. Even if it is just a little runt of a tree, it's a place to sleep."

When Merle awakened the next morning, he was so surprised he nearly tumbled off the branch. And what a tumble it would have been! The fog had drifted away and Merle discovered he was high in the air, up in the very tip top of a gigantic redwood! And on every side were more towering trees! A whole forest of them!

"I can't believe it," cried Merle, "I'm here! I'm here! I'm way out west in the big trees!"

"Like the man said," chortled the happy squirrel, "they *are* as tall as a building and a whole lot more beautiful. And there *is* a great quietness about them. And I *do* feel mighty small out here. But not measly small like I did in the city. It *is* a good feeling. Just great!"